I0591906

Poetry And The

Like

From The Mind

Of William Malave

I would like to give a fair warning that some of the content within these stories contains scenes/concepts of death, torture, alcohol abuse, physical abuse, mental stress, and suicide. All of these stories are fictional, and the ideas within them are meant to be read, not reenacted. Enjoy!

Copyright © 2020 William Malave

All rights reserved.

978-0-578-83649-2

Cover Art Designed by ShiviDesign (Barbara Maj)

Self-published by William Tyrese Malave, printed by IngramSpark.

Characters and Fantasies

The Beginning Of The Mask

Lavish meals and an awesome antiquity,

These words help manifest the unfathomable home of an arrogant

noble.

Countless hours spent on trivial challenges of intellect.

Years of his life wasted to a balding, faded shadow, and an old

curvaceous figure.

But the *swordsman*!

Day in and day out, the practice of the art consumed him.

Even the damnable creatures that raided his home didn't stand their

ground against his unwavering lust for combat.

The old man and woman were split in two, having succumbed to the

blight of indignity.

All of the guards and servants were brutalized, their bodies decorating

the already grim manor grounds.

The children were arranged in a pattern around the shattered

fountain, aside from one missing body.

The noble took to fixing the shape, and as he set the final body in

place, he heard the sound of screams erupt from the lifeless cadavers.

Their corpses rapidly decayed and their souls dripped with blood as

they gathered above the circle and mumbled dark hymns.

Then the shape split in two, tearing apart the miniature skeletons and the ravaged stone way.

The hand had reached the gate.

The Shack And The Storm

The door was slammed shut, culling the howling wind and entrapping the poor souls within.

Heavy breaths emanated from around the room, as the weary travelers huddled close together.

Their leader, a masked man wearing common clothes and a bit of armor upon his left shoulder, began to create a fire.

After the fire was made, the group sat together and began their dreaded wait for the storm's end.

An hour passed, and the fire was dwindling. The man watched the children before him, all four of them holding each other close, attempting to ward off the cold.

The shack was riddled with apertures, through which small gusts of death wandered toward the crackling flame.

There were three empty boxes within the room, and a frozen well outside.

The roof was heavily damaged, and the snow could be seen through the cracks in the ceiling.

The air was freezing.

By the time the man had added the last bit of wood to the fire, his arms and legs were already numb, and the children had almost turned blue.

One of them lay up against a box, separated from the rest as he stared blankly at the leftmost wall.

The heat began to wade, and the man began to tear at his shirt, feeding the flames with his scraps.

The kids were even closer to the fire now, letting the flames just barely touch their skin.

The wind picked up.

Another hour later, and the storm had started to tear at the wooden walls, picking away bits of the squatters' salvation.

The man was down to a couple of scraps of cloth where his trousers used to be, and yet only two children remained, one holding the other, who lay still upon the floor.

The flame was almost gone, and he could not save them.

He held his hand out to the weeping child, and she took it, embracing the man and holding on to him with the remainder of her strength.

The cold seemed to grow stronger, and the fire was down to a few scattered embers.

The little girl held close to his naked body, searching for some sort of warmth.

He held her tight, humming softly through his mask and whispering sweet nothings to her.

The wind slowed, and they waited.

When her grip fell loose, he lay her down with the other children, and silently left the building with his rugged belongings in hand.

With a final, shallow breath, the shack was left behind, and a single tear fell down his darkened face, although the wind took it before he could cherish it.

The Wickers

The forest was shrouded in darkness.

Shadows moved between the trees, and a faded whisper indulged his bloodied ears.

The clothless man entered the dark greenery, sealing his fate, holding tight his sword and mask.

His shoulder pad, alongside his briefs, were the only sources of clothing he had, and the snow still fell gently upon the dirt before him.

It was midday, but in the forest, the sun held no authority, only visible if the trees decided it.

This he knew as truth.

This he knew as scripture, written by his apathetic father, witnessed by his heretical mother.

For it read:

"Upon the fifth day, when the storm has quelled, and the rain, sleet, and snow have receded into the murky heavens above, the forest will peel itself open, free of the spells that bound it.

Several men will enter the forest, yet only three will exit, one for each pedestal of the altar.

The rest will have been slain by the Wickers, and their bodies seized by the earthen grasp of the endless trees.

The undignified cannot be allowed to exit the forest, for if he does, the monster will take its claim upon Quivona, and our precious world will be doomed to bleed into the sea of despair and hate that lies below us.

He can not reach the gate."

There was a fork, with one direction leading deeper into the forest, and the other littered with footprints, old and new. Most of the footprints were pressed deep into the ground, imprinted as if they were being pushed down by something heavy.

They were armored, clad in iron plate.

He took the path of footprints, gripping his sword tighter as he held it on his shoulders.

The trees watched him as he went, the soft clicks of the Wickers audible in every direction. Even above, where only the crowns of the trees were visible.

Their echoes spread through the forest like wild flame.

Twenty men, their faces shrouded in iron veils, standing before a large archway of cooked trees and corpses.

Just beyond their iron bodies, and the piles of dead, he saw the golden gate, in all of its malevolent glory.

The three pedestals were manned by the three, their bodies bare for the ancient to partake of.

The iron men stood facing him, his body half-naked, his mask shrouding his face, his sword settled upon his two shoulders, one of bronze and the other of iron.

"The undignified." His hammer fell to the ground with a heavy *thud*, scattering dust into the humid air.

The rest gathered around him, swords and shields raised, crossbows aimed.

The pedestals were lit with fire.

The fight lasted two minutes.

His sword carved through body after body, chopping limbs, stabbing through torsos.

He was now against the hammer holder, alone.

His hammer swung wide and heavy, arcing through the air until it eventually hit the dodging body, breaking his rib cage and causing horrid cries of anguish.

His sword swung back, splitting the wooden handhold in half, and slicing into the warrior's armor.

But the warrior used the hammer itself, swerving through the masked warrior's attacks and landing a devastating hit onto his mask, shattering it in two.

He slammed his hammer down again, breaking the warrior's knee, and releasing more cries of pain.

He did the same to his right arm, breaking the elbow first, and then the hand for good measure.

He lifted the masked warrior's sword and used it to cleave off the good leg, severing it in one blow.

Then he took the other leg, dropped the sword, and spit onto the exposed face.

"Weak." He spoke one word, but it meant everything to the downed warrior, who lay there, broken and defeated.

The remainder of his mask fell to the ground, exposing his full face, in all of it's scarred glory.

He let himself cry, feeling the sting of salt on blood, and the release of fluid from his open thighs.

His body ached.

He was exhausted, worn thin from failure.

His eyes wandered to the man with the hammer, who stood over his fallen men, praying to his god.

The masked warrior gathered what little strength he had, and crawled towards a fallen blade.

He could feel every ounce of blood trail behind him.

His bruised hand barely gripped the handle, but it would be enough.

He tucked it behind himself, and hacked up blood and vomit, drawing his attention.

The hammer holder walked over to him, holding his broken weapon, ready to end his prey.

"The undignified, brought low-" the blade pierced his neck, and he gagged and grasped for the handle, failing and falling to the ground.

The broken warrior slowly crawled through the crooked exit, staring at the three corpses, burned to the bone for the ancient.

He clawed through the dirt and grass, reaching the first of many steps. Once he struggled up to the top step, his body gave out, and he could no longer force himself to move.

The gate was before him, a golden circle of hate, sewn into the ground to summon evil.

He watched as the ash from the fires fell gently onto the gate, settling within the creases of the gold.

A heavy noise, like the opening of a metal door, or the encasement of a dragon, erupted from the golden exit.

Then it appeared, the giant hand, mangled, imbued with malignant power, far greater than anything of his wretched world.

He watched helplessly as the creature rose, the hand being shadowed by a monstrous body, a torso flayed and burned, arms encrusted in bloody gold, legs thicker than tree trunks, feet calloused, beaten, scorched.

Entiya, the demon's wife, abused, bloodied, and angry.

She bellowed, spitting fire and destruction, razing the forests, all except the Wickers, who had skittered their way to the side of the masked warrior.

They carried him into their untouched woodland, hanging him up on a tree with nails and deadwood. They wrapped leaves around his wounds and left him there, where he would hang for years, as their undignified offering, to their new god.

The Tree

A tree stands tall above a barren waste.

Several stumps, branches, and the like, marked the remnants of his fallen brethren.

Open fields used to cover the land, but they had waited too long for an ungiving nourishment.

Life-sustaining rivers flowed from the beautiful waterfall.

Every living creature in the forest would come to drink, satisfying themselves and giving offerings to the trees, whose roots were long since rotten.

Many years ago there was peace, and *equality*, among the forest folk.

None would enter the ever-expanding greenery of the Nook.

Gone. All of it lay to rest among the tree's dying roots.

Rails were placed alongside the water's old pathway.

Open fields turned into lodgings, made up of his family and friends.

Weapons were created from their branches.

Long before the coming of man, it was peaceful, happy even. But even a tree must stand up for itself, and its people, even if the men were stronger. Soon they will hear it.

Darkness And Deceit

A Faded Blue Collar

The Inn was full of rowdy banter and games of intellect, cherished by luck and indignation.

Several minutes had passed before he entered the place, his presence bringing forth a mist of death and agony.

The room became a chamber of torture and malformed monstrosities.

Screams filled the air, along with the thick must of drunken fools and prolonged temptations.

The man sat down at the bar, silently filling his tankard with ale as the innkeeper impaled himself with shards of glass, wailing as his eyes bled.

The man sipped his drink and took his leave, sending the Inn back into its trance-like state.

The drunken fools were crying tears of joy, and the innkeeper continued to remove shards of glass from the wooden floor.

The games continued merrily, and the yelling was louder than before.

As he emptied his pail into the murky bin, the innkeeper noticed a piece of blue cloth, though the color was faded and the texture worn.

A forlorn tusk of ivory was embedded at the rightmost tuft of ripped fur.

He lifted the collar from the shelf it was left upon, and inspected it silently.

A rap against his counter startled him, and he hid the curious thing in his back pocket.

His mind quickly set to mixing a concoction, allowing him to forget the object upon his person.

The night was cold and dark, and his clothing was heavy with his sweat.

The innkeeper succumbed to exhaustion, gently laying down on a time-tested bench.

He relaxed, his body slowly fading to sleep until he heard a noise that scared him half to death.

It was that of a child, screaming in agony.

He jumped up from the bench and searched for the source of the wailing. As he neared the woods the crying grew louder, and he jumped into the shrubbery without hesitation.

The surrounding trees were still, and the birds had stopped their conversations.

The insects were bothersome, but otherwise a minor nuisance in his search for the distressed child.

His eyes caught glimpse of a silhouette before an inordinate oak.

The Innkeep, tired and rather angry at the disturbance, called out to the child, whose cries had been sedated a bit earlier in his trek.

But the figure did not turn. It only sobbed in it's lonesome.

As he approached the lost child, he began to see more of the figure's appearance.

Its hair was long and straight, like that of a noble.

It was unusual for it's tattered clothing and peasant-like hunch.

His eyes followed the arched back to shoeless feet, of which the nails were grimy and green.

He called to the child once more, and it responded with a resounding crack of it's back.

It screamed, bellowing a monstrous noise as it's contorted frame made way for the Innkeep.

He cried out as he ran from the creature, whose feet made noises that could not be described.

Then, the chase suddenly stopped, and the Innkeep quickly turned to see where it had gone.

But there was no trace of the thing, aside from a bloody journal embedded into a nearby tree.

His journey home had been one of horror, though his mind tried to make sense of what he'd seen as he carried home that forsaken object and its counterpart, the bloody journal.

Passerbys offered him wares and rations, but he politely refused, claiming he just needed to get home.

He entered his established manor, immediately being greeted by his enthusiastic child, whom he hugged and kissed.

From the kitchen, he could hear his wife humming a quaint gospel, and he silently listened as he climbed his oaken stairway.

He entered his bathroom, removing his filthy clothes and cleansing himself with soap and water within the basin.

Once he finished cleaning himself, he hefted his clothes into the washroom, where he hand-washed his apparel, within each pocket and button, scrubbing out every bit of grime and dirt.

As he cleaned his coat, he came upon the journal, which he also cleaned before he shifted his focus.

He sat on a nearby stool and peeled back the sticky pages, revealing one single page of writing, titled "From Bar, To Wood, To Table."

There was no author.

It read:

His ire was strong and constant.

His will to work reluctant.

His kindness forged from falsehoods.

His fill of duty forsaken to the woods.

Tempted as he was, he persevered.

He was able to reach his shack.

But alas he was not truly there,

Amongst blood sat those whose love he lacked.

His wife was bled from head to toe,

His son decapitated amongst a fable,

His life was stolen from below,

And done before he reached the table.

The Innkeep wiped a steady tear from his face, feeling a faint resonance with the unnamed character.

He searched the rest of the journal, but to his surprise, the rest of the pages were filled with nonsense.

He left the washroom to eat his dinner, which sat prepared for him at the table.

His wife laughed as he hugged her, and told her about his day. But before he sat, she told him to fetch their son.

He made his way back up the stairs, his mind stuck to the poem.

He opened his son's door and found him dead, his head removed from his leaking neck, and his storybook dripping with blood.

He sobbed as he ran down his stairs, fumbling about the rotted railing and broken steps.

He fell to the floor and landed on a rat, whom he squished beneath his tattered trousers.

He entered his kitchen, the cabinets dangling by the handles and the sunlight lazily peeking through a single, boarded window.

His wife was torn in two, her insides spilled about the floorboards and leading down a narrow hole.

And there on the table, infested with bugs, was his dinner, and alongside it, a faded blue collar.

A Simple Trinket

Her sword was cleaved through the final creature, splitting its torso from its waist, spilling vile blood upon the cobblestone ground.

She sighed, her body aching and her head on fire.

All she could think of was a drink.

She let herself collapse on the ground, resting on one of the many beast corpses around her.

It smelt of dog and piss, but its skin was smooth like a sanded stone.

She closed her golden eyes, listening to the critters crawl about, to the slight shimmer of gold in the room.

She opened an eye, looking to her left where a single, shining stone revealed itself.

She sat up with a grunt, removing a thin spike of stone from her thigh, letting blood trickle down her leg.

The stone was extraordinary, but it had a presence to it, one of death and misery.

It in itself seemed to have power beyond her control, and it smelled like must.

She pocketed it and left the room.

The city was full of merchants and vagrants, yet her goal was to meet a

particular vendor, one who collected and sold items of intrigue.

She wandered past an old inn, and could practically taste the rum

from the outside.

Her temptations called her, and she turned onto its wooden pathway.

Then she was hit with a wave of exhaustion, so sudden that she almost

fell over.

She held her head, feeling around her pocket for the stone, which was

buzzing like a wasp.

It vibrated within her hands, sending shivers through her body.

She decided that the drinks would wait until she'd gotten rid of the

thing.

Along the forest road, every animal within touching distance snarled

at her, as if she were some sort of threat.

The buzzing had stopped, but she felt a slight aberration every time

she strayed from the beaten path.

She felt that the stone held some sort of power, which only further led

her to the collector's solitary home.

A bear wandered across the road, staring at her as it did so.

It's teeth bared for a second, and then it ran off as if scared of a single

woman in peasant's clothes.

The stone did not buzz until she'd reached his home.

The stone hut was broken, cracked along every side and angle,

billowing smoke from a dilapidated chimney.

The windows were barely held together by sticks and pebbles, and the

door was covered in slick mildew.

She rapped against the sodden wood, flicking globs of the stuff onto

the ground as he opened the door, ecstatic.

His eyes were wild with excitement as he hurried her in and made her

show him the stone.

When he saw it he looked like a child who'd found candy.

Without any haggling, he offered most of his coin, enough for her to

buy a home of her own.

Then he hurried her out of his home and slammed the door.

She shrugged and made way for the road, just barely hearing the

screams from behind her.

A sudden must filled the air, sickening her instantly, invoking vomit

and a clenched jaw.

She forced herself inside his home, to see a figure, not unlike a man,

holding the collector by his neck.

She drew her sword, only to be met by his steel eyes and another wave

of nausea and vomiting.

He obtained some sort of information from the collector, as the last thing she heard were desperate pleas and a resounding snap of bone.

When she woke, she was outside, surrounded by dead grass and animals.

The trees of the forest were misshaped, crooked even, and the road was littered with corpses of birds and rodents.

She stood on uneasy legs and forced herself to walk along with the horrors of the path.

The bear was split in two, it's insides sprawled about and surrounded by dead rats and crows.

Even the insects had died upon the blood-soaked gravel.

She made her way to the inn, where the lights were dark and the pathway had eroded a bit on the stone parts.

Past the inn the market was quiet.

All of the vendors had retreated indoors, and the vagrants were nestled within their makeshift tents.

As she walked she began to feel the stone again, its painful hum.

She followed the smell to an old shack, with shattered windows and bloodied footprints trailing from the steps down the street.

She peeked inside, seeing three corpses by a broken dinner table.

There was a woman, a headless child, and a man with a gun still held tight in his cold grasp.

She followed the footsteps, wavering as the stench became more and more fragrant.

Then the trail ended, just before the church.

She pried open the door, finding the source of the blockage.

Corpses of priests and townsfolk alike, their bodies mangled like a witch's play dolls.

She stared straight ahead at the figure, who kneeled before a dark sphere in the room.

As she entered, the sphere disappeared into the air, and the figure stood and turned to face her.

She drew her sword, eyeing the bodies of her fellow mercenaries, whose armor was torn to shreds as if it was paper.

The figure slowly walked towards her, releasing the same vile stench as it did in the collector's home.

She rushed forward, attempting to suppress the smell with her rags, only to feel it seep through like murky water.

As she reached striking distance, the aroma grew stronger, forcing her to her knees.

She expelled vomit until her body felt too weak to persist.

She fought the feeling of weakness and lunged for the being's throat.

She missed, but her sword grazed the side of his face, spilling a mossy goo onto the hardwood.

It made no noise, had no reaction.

It only stared at the woman before it.

She suddenly felt an extreme wave of pain, which rushed throughout her body until it reached her head.

She cried and screamed, clawing at her face until blood was drawn, peeling her skin like the pain peeled her brain.

She could feel her entire body ripping itself apart until her spine snapped in half, and her skull caved in on itself, leaving her body mangled like the rest.

What Lurks

It is a three-minute walk, from my home to the main road.

The pathway is a dirt road, littered with old candy wrappers and a few lost possessions.

On either side of the dirt road was woodland, with trees tall enough to blot out the sun.

On that darkened path I walked, listening silently to the birds, and the buzzing insects.

The bugs loved to swarm certain areas of the path but tended not to leave their feed.

Some trees had scratches on them, old knicks from their past transgressions with people.

The dirt itself seemed hardened in the wake of sodden shoes, constant walking, and scattered litter.

But it cannot defend itself.

Not on it's own.

I only had two minutes left in my walk, and I could just barely see the lights of passing cars.

Their noise was irritating, the constant mechanical hum.

It wasn't as peaceful as the bugs were, they were natural, unfiltered.

My feet began to grow weary, and I quickly stopped to massage them.

They felt dry, almost as if the skin would peel away like old plaster.

They had recently been thoroughly scrubbed, after their laborious abuse.

I sighed and kept walking, resetting my torn sock and fixing my broken shoes.

I rolled my shoulders a bit, feeling the tensity release itself like a wave of calm.

They were sore from the day's work, and my shirt had many rips and tears to show for it.

I had covered it with my favorite sweater, although there was little improvement.

I hadn't completely finished dyeing it my favorite color.

I only had a minute left.

It felt like it had been hours.

I could hear nothing among the woods anymore.

All of the birds were still, the bugs had stopped buzzing, and the trees silently watched me.

I was joyous every time I reached the end of the path.

My loneliness would be lost from me, just for a while.

I could finally see people.

I scratched my back pocket, itching past the stubborn hilt.

I cracked my neck, easing the knots from last night, and pushing up my collar to hide my bruised neck.

I smiled to myself, proud of my dedication, to my honed focus.

My therapist always told me that for people like me, it was hard to make friends.

But I always disagreed and would tell her that I did have many friends.

I had plenty of relationships.

I had made it.

The road was empty, and the trees behind it listened in. Everything around me listened in.

I could feel the bugs behind me, crawling up my back and resting on my shoulders.

The birds were sitting upon their perches, curiously watching for the headlights like I was.

The trees, with all of their horrible scars and insults for humanity, still would watch *me* work.

They all liked me, even though they despised everyone else.

Then they came.

Their dual brightness like a sign from god.

I waved down the car, and it stopped, rolling down its precious glass and revealing what I had been searching for.

"Hey, buddy you lost?" He asked me, with a genuine look of pure, total innocence.

I smiled a warm, toothy grin.

I stared into those scarless eyes, and answered, "Yes, I need a ride."

In The Nook Of A Tree

Eight, thirteen, nineteen-twenty three.

The day I die.

I remember being cradled by a woman.

Whether or not she was my mother is irrelevant.

At least, I believe so.

She wore sunglasses and a wide-brimmed hat.

Her mouth was covered in red lipstick, smeared along top and bottom.

Her clothes were torn, the animal fur of her coat down to a few strands.

Her gown, reduced to a skirt and torn at the chest, exposing deflated breasts.

Her skin was shriveled and peeling. She was not unlike a zombie.

Her knees were bruised, and her ankles were swollen.

Her feet were disgustingly dry, and the toenails were covered in grime.

She would never touch me, much less hold me.

But that one instance, just for a moment, she held me, like a true mother.

And then she dropped me.

My head was cracked along the back. Blood and a sort of grayish mucus leaked from it.

I did not cry. I did not whine. I only bled. This is not how I died.

I remember a man.

His smile was vacant.

His eyes were soulless.

His face was rugged, but not handsomely.

His left ear was missing. I had never felt better.

His right leg was shattered and hung about his pelvis like a dead animal.

His back was slit down the middle, The scar deep and sickly. I laughed at him.

His nose was crooked.

His forehead was wrinkled.

His hair was ripped from his scalp. I hated him.

I will not confess.

His feet were bloodied and oozing. The toenails were removed.

His arms were cut along the veins. I loved him.

His mouth was sewn shut.

His cheeks were riddled with miniature holes.

His fingers lacked skin.

His chest was caved in.

His wife was unhappy.

His son...

His happiness was long removed.

His features were gone.

I will not confess.

I remember a building.

The windows were broken, sealed by rusty nails and rotted wood.

The stairs lacked steps, and the railing was peeled away by the bugs.

The floors were cracked apart and littered with trapped glass. I
remember the vase.

The walls contained empty picture frames. The paper was ash used for
kindling.

The stove was rusted and infested with corpses of rodents.

The cabinets were missing handles, and void of cutlery and platters.

The television was static, wherever the screen remained.

The couch was stained with past affairs and unwashed clothing.

The curtains were chewed upon. One of my last dinners.

The bathroom was stained with blood. So much of it was mine.

The woman had thrown me in the sink and rinsed me of her sins.

Her hands were dirtied and her breaths were ragged.

The man was hollering, creaking back and forth with his inconceivable
laugh.

My arms, flailed about as they were, lay limp along the sides of the sink.

My legs were rid of their skin, revealing the pink of my inner being.

The blood. It was only blood.

So many of my clothes were drowned in the toilet, along with the mice.

My eye was grimy, stained a fearsome black from the stove's flames.

The legless dog silently licked my remains from the piss-stained tiles.

This is not how I died.

My final memory rests within the nook of a tree.

Gruesome as it may seem,

The memory wasn't me.

My body never made it to the nook of that tree.

A string, I believe one of the laces of my soleless shoe, hung from a stubborn branch.

Upon that lace was the man, his neck wrung tight and his body limp.

He couldn't run fast enough from me, his wheelchair forbade it.

I confess I killed my father.

He was the first of my sins.

My mother watched and cried, but not for him, for her greatest feat.

A murderous devil of a son.

My mother threw my father's wheelchair into a nearby tree.

There were plenty of them among the woods.

The metal seat fell to pieces and laid to rest in the reddened earth.

My mother held me, embraced me even. She lifted me and cradled me.

My eyes were moist with tears. I had never known my heart.

The way her body sank, as I ripped her face apart.

My blade was quick to start,

My nails made gruesome art.

Her eyes welled with bloodied tears, and I screamed as they kissed my face.

I took her torn flesh, and my father's ghastly teeth,

And I tucked them nice and neat, into the nook, of a tree.

The Window

The man asked me if I was afraid.

Of course, I answered no.

To instill fear, for a year, he really should have more to show.

I'm a fading whisper of a soul, and my remaining days number low.

But I have yet, any respect, for his unrelenting serenade.

The man asked if I was hungry.

Of course, I answered yes.

He starved me, and he scarred me, made my cell a filthy mess.

I was once free of this prison, an everyday citizen.

But I digress, yes, I confess, I am a sinner to my country.

The man asked about my wife.

Of course, I said she hated me.

For a year, I'd disappeared, and never again, would I be free.

I miss my dear daughter, who thinks I've drowned underwater.

But my family, and my sanity, were lost to this life.

The man asked if I wished to be free.

Of course, I said yes.

For the shackles to be undone, by anyone, I wanted nothing less.

I loathed to be home, never again alone.

But as it stands, my reprimands will never let me be.

The man asked if I could see beyond the bedrock.

Of course, I answered no.

Behind a window, stood a shadow, a face I'd never know.

I must've had his words misconstrued. Never before had I been so entirely confused.

But I heard a clicking, a quick ticking, the releasing of my lock.

For a moment, he was silent.

And I was silent too.

He knew that I was violent.

He knew what I could do.

Yet my shackles released easy.

My freedom, beyond the glass.

I stood and felt uneasy.

For a year I'd been on my ass.

The walls were made of rocks.

The glass was hard as steel.

There was a bucket filled with socks.

And an old banana peel.

I banged my fist on the window.

And then I banged it more.

I let out a wild bellow,

My rage an angry roar.

I lifted my metal chair and took it to the glass.

One hit made a *bang!*

Another made a *crash!*

As the glass fell to the floor,

And my rage began to quell,

My mind sank to horror,

As I entered another cell.

Martyr

We gather around this decadent flame to expose true blasphemy.

His conviction is that of heresy, betrayal of his people and his cause.

Yet we do not intend to relieve poor Reli of his time-held vessel.

Through arduous trials, we have come to realize Reli's true power as a martyr.

He shall be held high above the Irlyn border, atop the Silver Chapel.

Everyone, join me, as we carry his unholy body to a hopeful sanctuary.

We shall now recite our lord's holy orders, written upon the earthen tombstone of our father.

Among the rebellious people of Teper and Lovil, we shall discover a grand being.

Time will eventually overtake us, and before we are reborn we shall sacrifice this being.

Every man, woman, and child of Irlyn shall stand and watch as the man is persecuted.

Ready yourselves for my final verdict.

Reli looked down at the thousands of people who held torches and cradled their loved ones.

Unknown feelings enclosed him within a dark sphere, blocking his vision of everything.

Nothing could be heard or seen among the darkness, aside from a woman with long red hair.

She let her hair fall to her smooth feet, and wrap around her naked body. She beckoned him.

Reli let his hand escape his will, and attempted to reach the woman, but his grasp felt nothing.

Everything returned to normal, and he felt a wave of air push against him. He heard screams.

During his fall temptation took hold of him, and he let his body float towards a jagged rock.

All of the Irlyn people screamed in horror as Reli's body was impaled by the rock.

Gore hung around the edges, and blood trickled into the dark river.

Animals cried out in agony, the plants withered to gray filth and the water stopped flowing.

Imperfect spires formed around his corpse and were flocked by blood-red birds.

Negligent souls howled as they fled their decaying bodies, leaving withered scraps for the vultures.

Release

The Ladder

Some say the ladder is a hundred feet high.

The woman let out a sigh.

The crowd around her was not shy.

They grabbed at her, cheering, waving their hands, saying hi.

Her eyes sadly stared, a tear welling in her eye.

The ladder was a long climb, and she had no time to cry.

She gathered her courage, her fear now awry.

She started climbing, unsure she'd make it, but determined to try.

It continued upward, peg by peg, she didn't want to lie.

But of course, knowing her, she never said goodbye.

Her husband watched as she left, his name was Malachi.

He kissed her, said he'd miss her, he was a good guy.

She said it was Vegas, but by now, he would've checked to verify.

The helicopter buzzed by.

It watched her, as she climbed, annoying as a fly.

The top of the wall was visible, she could see the end was nigh.

Her dreams were coming true, she'd thought her luck had run dry.

Then her feet were on top, and she could see the earth behind.

Her mind became at peace, and for a moment, she wondered why.

As she fell from the top, knowing she would die.

Abyss

But the water was gorgeous.

It was her only thought.

Perfectly natural, and the waves were so smooth.

The orange birds skimmed the water, and beautiful streaks followed their stride.

No ships were allowed to sail, but a few would stand on the shore, like her, their toes wiggling in the gentle touch of warm water.

Her eyes wandered and met another woman, who sat next to her and tilted her head back, a smooth pink smile bringing out her dimples.

The woman sat with her, and the two watched the waves together.

After a moment the two stood and lay back against the water, letting it take them away from the crystalline shore and ever-still statues.

She watched as the city slowly faded away, all of her life, left on the shore.

She let her eyes softly close, as exhaustion gripped her.

Her mind ran empty, and her breathing became shallow.

She could feel her body relaxing more, and more until she couldn't feel that woman's smooth fingers against her side.

Her body slowly sunk into the water, her mind free, her soul gently escaping her fading grasp, and melodically humming a beautiful hymn.

Her body was left empty, a fruitless vessel, floating amidst the beautiful city.

Young River

How he talked, was like a poet, Young River.

How he walked was like a king, Young River.

How he stared was like a dreamer, Young River.

How he glared was like a monster, Young River.

How the flowers would bloom when he touched them.

How the rain would settle, where he strode.

How his eyes could calm storms

How his breath could ease soldiers

This man, was different, Young River.

How his mind was always clear, and decisive.

How his skin was bronze, and intuitive

How his beauty was unrivaled, and invited

This man, was our winner, Young River.

How he cried, when she passed, Young River.

How he simply, was unhappy, Young River.

How he fought, and was distraught, Young River.

This angel, is no longer, Young River.

Of An Angel, And a Wing

My eyes are not my own, as she said.

My body is a temple, pure and simple.

Yet my mirror never shatters in my stead.

Live long, Live wild, Be happy.

A motto, folklore, for the weary.

Never brought below indulgence.

Given freely for those who want it.

Unless otherwise, it was taken.

Another one, stolen.

Given as a token.

Even my gratitude precedes me.

But I am as I am.

Broken and battered, but not lost to its rhythm.

It's hum and resonance, deep and strong within my weakened heart.

I am one with my speech, as I am one, with my end.

Now I am released, to be free of this test.

A Note From Me To You

I never would have thought that at some point, I would have something of mine put out into the world. To have my ideas and crazy thoughts shared abroad is an incredible feeling to me, and I hope that whoever reads this finds something they like, because God knows there's a variety of things in here. After all is said and done, I am happy that I get to share my strangest thoughts with the world, and I hope someone, or you, enjoys them as much as I enjoyed writing them. Thank you, not just for coming this far and hopefully enjoying yourself, but for making a dream of mine come true.

www.ingramcontent.com/pod-product-compliance
Lightning Source LLC
Chambersburg PA
CBHW070402120726
47909CB00008B/2965